MOON MAN

Phaidon Press Limited
Regent's Wharf
All Saints Street
London N1 9PA

Phaidon Press Inc.
180 Varick Street
New York, NY 10014

www.phaidon.com

This edition © 2009 Phaidon Press Limited
First published in German as *Der Mondmann*
© 1966 Diogenes Verlag AG Zürich

ISBN 978 0 7148 5598 1

A CIP catalogue record for this book is
available from the British Library.

Printed in China

MOON MAN

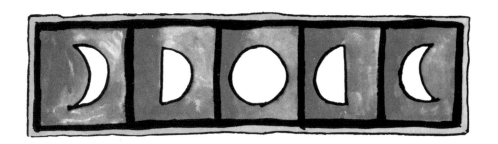

TOMI UNGERER

On clear, starry nights the Moon Man can be seen
curled up in his shimmering seat in space.

Every night from his drifting sphere, the Moon Man was
filled with envy as he watched the earth people dance.
"If only once I could join the fun," he thought.
"Life up here is such a bore."

One night a shooting star
flashed by. The Moon Man
leaped just in time to catch the
fiery tail of the comet.

The night creatures of the woods fled in terror at the loud crash of the fallen star.

The noise brought hundreds of people from a nearby town. Soldiers sped to defend the earth. Firemen hastened to quench the flaming light. The ice cream man hurried to set up his stand for the spectators.

When they reached the site of the crash, no one could decide what the pale, soft creature lying in the crater could be.

Government officials were alerted.

Statesmen, scientists, and generals panicked.

They called the mysterious visitor an invader.

The Moon Man was thrown in jail while a special court
conducted a criminal investigation. Poor Moon Man . . .
his hopes of dancing among the merry crowds and bright
lanterns were crushed.

One night as the Moon Man sat wondering why he was so
cruelly treated, he noticed that his left side had faded.
"Why, I must be in my third quarter," he thought happily.
Every night as the moon grew thinner and thinner so did the
Moon Man, until at last he was able to squeeze through the
bars of his window.

When the head of the armed forces paid a visit to inspect the weird captive, he found the cell empty. The general was furious.

Days later, as the moon reappeared in its first quarter,
a quarter of the Moon Man came back. Two weeks later
he had reached his full size again.

Delighted with his freedom, he wandered about,

discovering the sweet-smelling flowers,

the splendid birds and butterflies.

He came upon a garden party where people in gorgeous costumes were dancing. "Look! Someone has come as the man in the moon," a lady cried. The Moon Man danced blissfully for hours.

Alas, a grumpy killjoy complained of the late music
to the police. Scared by the sight of the guns and uniforms,

the Moon Man dashed off to the nearby woods.

But he was spotted by the policemen, and a wild chase began.

Swiftly outracing the police, the Moon Man shot across the countryside. In a lonely place he came upon an ancient castle.

There he was welcomed by a long-forgotten scientist,

Doktor Bunsen van der Dunkel. For centuries he had

been perfecting a spacecraft to reach the moon.

Now finished, the intricate machine rested on its launch
pad in a castle turret. Doktor van der Dunkel had grown too
old and too fat to fit into the capsule. He asked his guest to
be his first passenger. The Moon Man, who had realized that
he could never live peacefully on this planet, agreed to go.

Doktor van der Dunkel decided to wait for the moon to enter its third quarter. "By then the Moon Man will have grown small enough to fit into the capsule," he thought. A few nights later, the Moon Man took leave of his benefactor. With tears in their eyes they bade each other farewell. Then the Moon Man blasted off with a roar of rockets.

Having succeeded in the launching of his spacecraft, Doktor van der Dunkel at last received the recognition he had so long deserved. He was elected chairman of an important scientific committee.

Having satisfied his curiosity, the Moon Man never returned to earth
and remained ever after curled up in his shimmering seat in space.